Jeremy

# A
# Light
# in
# the
# Attic

# A Light in the Attic

# Shel Silverstein

HarperCollins*Publishers*

Library of Congress Catalog Card Number: 80-8453
ISBN 0-06-025673-7
ISBN 0-06-025674-5 (lib. bdg.)

## A LIGHT IN THE ATTIC

There's a light on in the attic.
Though the house is dark and shuttered,
I can see a flickerin' flutter,
And I know what it's about.
There's a light on in the attic.
I can see it from the outside,
And I know you're on the inside . . . lookin' out.

## HOW MANY, HOW MUCH

How many slams in an old screen door?
    Depends how loud you shut it.
How many slices in a bread?
    Depends how thin you cut it.
How much good inside a day?
    Depends how good you live 'em.
How much love inside a friend?
    Depends how much you give 'em.

## MOON-CATCHIN' NET

I've made me a moon-catchin' net,
And I'm goin' huntin' tonight,
I'll run along swingin' it over my head,
And grab for that big ball of light.

So tomorrow just look at the sky,
And if there's no moon you can bet
I've found what I sought and I finally caught
The moon in my moon-catchin' net.

But if the moon's still shinin' there,
Look close underneath and you'll get
A clear look at me in the sky swingin' free
With a star in my moon-catchin' net.

## HAMMOCK

Grandma sent the hammock,
The good Lord sent the breeze.
I'm here to do the swinging—
Now, who's gonna move the trees?

## HOW NOT TO HAVE
## TO DRY THE DISHES

If you have to dry the dishes
(Such an awful, boring chore)
If you have to dry the dishes
('Stead of going to the store)
If you have to dry the dishes
And you drop one on the floor—
Maybe they won't let you
Dry the dishes anymore.

## STOP THIEF!

Policeman, policeman,
Help me please.
Someone went and stole my knees.
I'd chase him down but I suspect
My feet and legs just won't connect.

## THE SITTER

Mrs. McTwitter the baby-sitter,
I think she's a little bit crazy.
She thinks a baby-sitter's supposed
To sit upon the baby.

14

## PRAYER OF THE SELFISH CHILD

Now I lay me down to sleep,
I pray the Lord my soul to keep,
And if I die before I wake,
I pray the Lord my toys to break.
So none of the other kids can use 'em. . . .
Amen.

## WHAT DID?

What did the carrot say to the wheat?
" 'Lettuce' rest, I'm feeling 'beet.' "
What did the paper say to the pen?
"I feel quite all 'write,' my friend."
What did the teapot say to the chalk?
Nothing, you silly . . . teapots can't talk!

I FEEL
ALL
WRITE

## SHAKING

Geraldine now, stop shaking that cow
For heaven's sake, for your sake and the cow's sake.
That's the dumbest way I've seen
To make a milk shake.

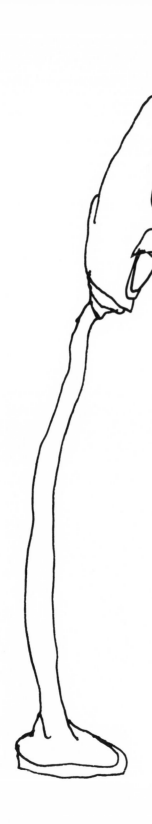

## SIGNALS

When the light is green you go.
When the light is red you stop.
But what do you do
When the light turns blue
With orange and lavender spots?

# PICTURE PUZZLE PIECE

One picture puzzle piece
Lyin' on the sidewalk,
One picture puzzle piece
Soakin' in the rain.
It might be a button of blue
On the coat of the woman
Who lived in a shoe.
It might be a magical bean,
Or a fold in the red
Velvet robe of a queen.
It might be the one little bite
Of the apple her stepmother
Gave to Snow White.
It might be the veil of a bride
Or a bottle with some evil genie inside.
It might be a small tuft of hair
On the big bouncy belly
Of Bobo the Bear.
It might be a bit of the cloak
Of the Witch of the West
As she melted to smoke.
It might be a shadowy trace
Of a tear that runs down an angel's face.
Nothing has more possibilities
Than one old wet picture puzzle piece.

## PUT SOMETHING IN

Draw a crazy picture,
Write a nutty poem,
Sing a mumble-gumble song,
Whistle through your comb.
Do a loony-goony dance
'Cross the kitchen floor,
Put something silly in the world
That ain't been there before.

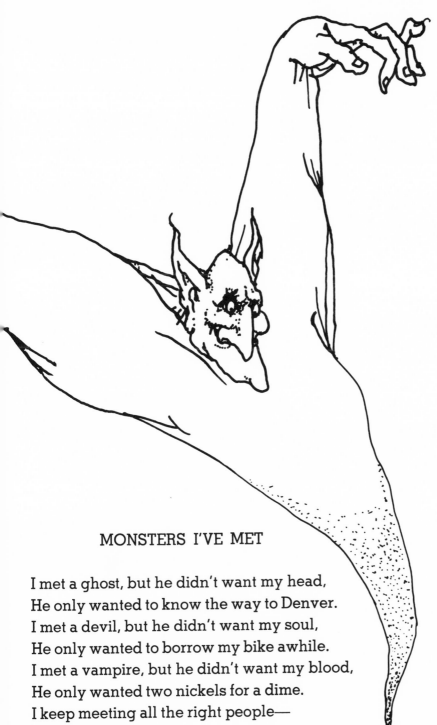

## MONSTERS I'VE MET

I met a ghost, but he didn't want my head,
He only wanted to know the way to Denver.
I met a devil, but he didn't want my soul,
He only wanted to borrow my bike awhile.
I met a vampire, but he didn't want my blood,
He only wanted two nickels for a dime.
I keep meeting all the right people—
At all the wrong times.

# ROCK 'N' ROLL BAND

If we were a rock 'n' roll band,
We'd travel all over the land.
We'd play and we'd sing and wear spangly things,
If we were a rock 'n' roll band.

If we were a rock 'n' roll band,
And we were up there on the stand,
The people would hear us and love us and cheer us,
Hurray for that rock 'n' roll band.

If we were a rock 'n' roll band,
Then we'd have a million fans.
We'd giggle and laugh and sign autographs,
If we were a rock 'n' roll band.

If we were a rock 'n' roll band,
The people would all kiss our hands.
We'd be millionaires and have extra long hair,
If we were a rock 'n' roll band.

But we ain't no rock 'n' roll band,
We're just seven kids in the sand
With homemade guitars and pails and jars
And drums of potato chip cans.

Just seven kids in the sand,
Talkin' and wavin' our hands,
And dreamin' and thinkin' oh wouldn't it be grand,
If we were a rock 'n' roll band.

## SOMETHING MISSING

I remember I put on my socks,
I remember I put on my shoes.
I remember I put on my tie
That was painted
In beautiful purples and blues.
I remember I put on my coat,
To look perfectly grand at the dance,
Yet I feel there is something
I may have forgot—
What is it? What is it? . . .

## MEMORIZIN' MO

Mo memorized the dictionary
But just can't seem to find a job
Or anyone who wants to marry
Someone who memorized the dictionary.

## SOMEBODY HAS TO

Somebody has to go polish the stars,
They're looking a little bit dull.
Somebody has to go polish the stars,
For the eagles and starlings and gulls
Have all been complaining they're tarnished and worn,
They say they want new ones we cannot afford.
So please get your rags
And your polishing jars,
Somebody has to go polish the stars.

## REFLECTION

Each time I see the Upside-Down Man
Standing in the water,
I look at him and start to laugh,
Although I shouldn't oughtter.
For maybe in another world
Another time
Another town,
Maybe HE is right side up
And I am upside down.

## FANCY DIVE

The fanciest dive that ever was dove
Was done by Melissa of Coconut Grove.
She bounced on the board and flew into the air
With a twist of her head and a twirl of her hair.
She did thirty-four jackknives, backflipped and spun,
Quadruple gainered, and reached for the sun,
And then somersaulted nine times and a quarter—
And looked down and saw that the pool had no water.

## HERE COMES

Here comes summer,
Here comes summer,
Chirping robin, budding rose.
Here comes summer,
Here comes summer,
Gentle showers, summer clothes.
Here comes summer,
Here comes summer—
Whoosh—shiver—there it goes.

## THE DRAGON OF GRINDLY GRUN

I'm the Dragon of Grindly Grun,
I breathe fire as hot as the sun.
When a knight comes to fight
I just toast him on sight,
Like a hot crispy cinnamon bun.

When I see a fair damsel go by,
I just sigh a fiery sigh,
And she's baked like a 'tater—
I think of her later
With a romantic tear in my eye.

I'm the Dragon of Grindly Grun,
But my lunches aren't very much fun,
For I like my damsels medium rare,
And they *always* come out well done.

# BLAME

I wrote such a beautiful book for you
'Bout rainbows and sunshine
And dreams that come true.
But the goat went and ate it
(You knew that he would),
So I wrote you another one
Fast as I could.
Of course it could never be
Nearly as great
As that beautiful book
That the silly goat ate.
So if you don't like
This new book I just wrote—
Blame the goat.

## MESSY ROOM

Whosever room this is should be ashamed!
His underwear is hanging on the lamp.
His raincoat is there in the overstuffed chair,
And the chair is becoming quite mucky and damp.
His workbook is wedged in the window,
His sweater's been thrown on the floor.
His scarf and one ski are beneath the TV,
And his pants have been carelessly hung on the door.
His books are all jammed in the closet,
His vest has been left in the hall.
A lizard named Ed is asleep in his bed,
And his smelly old sock has been stuck to the wall.
Whosever room this is should be ashamed!
Donald or Robert or Willie or—
Huh? You say it's mine? Oh dear,
I *knew* it looked familiar!

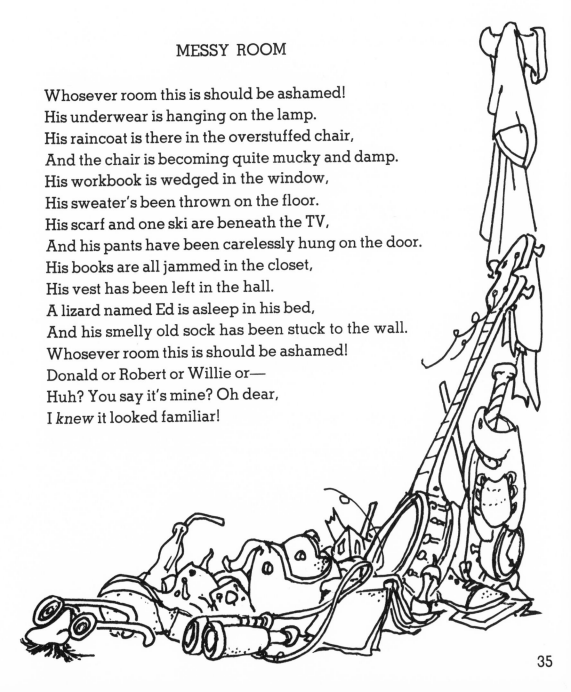

# NEVER

I've never roped a Brahma bull,
I've never fought a duel,
I've never crossed the desert
On a lop-eared, swayback mule,
I've never climbed an idol's nose
To steal a cursèd jewel.

I've never gone down with my ship
Into the bubblin' brine,
I've never saved a lion's life
And then had him save mine,
Or screamed Ahoooo while swingin' through
The jungle on a vine.

I've never dealt draw poker
In a rowdy lumber camp,
Or got up at the count of nine
To beat the world's champ,
I've never had my picture on
A six-cent postage stamp.

I've never scored a touchdown
On a ninety-nine-yard run,
I've never winged six Daltons
With my dying brother's gun . . .
Or kissed Miz Jane, and rode my hoss
Into the setting sun.
Sometimes I get so depressed
'Bout what I haven't done.

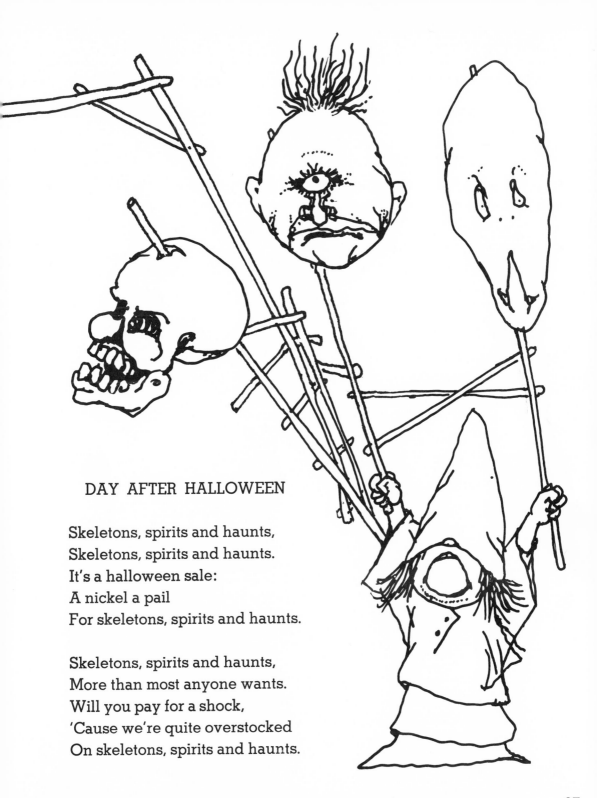

## DAY AFTER HALLOWEEN

Skeletons, spirits and haunts,
Skeletons, spirits and haunts.
It's a halloween sale:
A nickel a pail
For skeletons, spirits and haunts.

Skeletons, spirits and haunts,
More than most anyone wants.
Will you pay for a shock,
'Cause we're quite overstocked
On skeletons, spirits and haunts.

# WAVY HAIR

I thought that I had wavy hair
Until I shaved. Instead,
I find that I have *straight* hair
And a very wavy head.

## LONGMOBILE

It's the world's longest car, I swear,
It reaches from Beale Street to Washington Square.
And once you get in it
To go where you're going,
You simply get out, 'cause you're *there*.

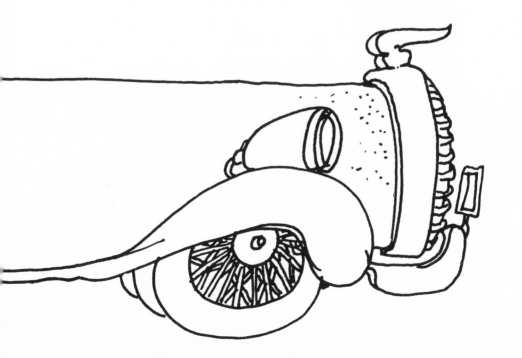

# BACKWARD BILL

Backward Bill, Backward Bill,
He lives way up on Backward Hill,
Which is really a hole in the sandy ground
(But that's a hill turned upside down).

Backward Bill's got a backward shack
With a big front porch that's built out back.
You walk through the window and look out the door
And the cellar is up on the very top floor.

Backward Bill he rides like the wind
Don't know where he's going but sees where he's been.
His spurs they go "neigh" and his horse it goes "clang,"
And his six-gun goes "gnab," it never goes "bang."

Backward Bill's got a backward pup,
They eat their supper when the sun comes up,
And he's got a wife named Backward Lil,
"She's my own true hate," says Backward Bill.

Backward Bill wears his hat on his toes
And puts on his underwear over his clothes.
And come every payday he pays his boss,
And rides off a-smilin' a-carryin' his hoss.

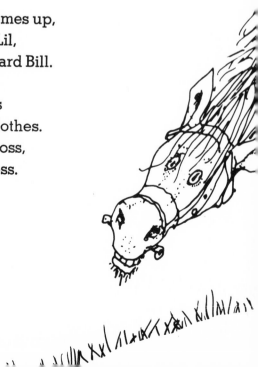

## MR. SMEDS AND MR. SPATS

Mr. Spats
Had twenty-one hats,
And none of them were the same.
And Mr. Smeds
Had twenty-one heads
And only one hat to his name.

Now, when Mr. Smeds
Met Mr. Spats,
They talked of the
Buying and selling of hats.
And Mr. Spats
Bought *Mr. Smeds'* hat!
Did you ever hear anything
Crazier than that?

## SNAKE PROBLEM

It's not that I don't care for snakes,
But oh what do you do
When a 24-foot python says . . .

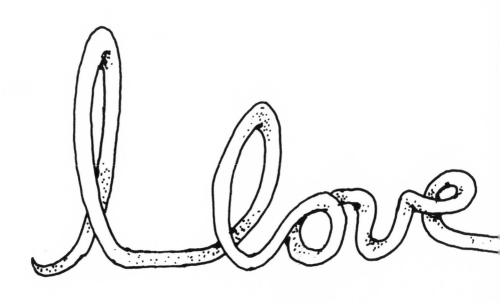

## BEAR IN THERE

There's a Polar Bear
In our Frigidaire—
He likes it 'cause it's cold in there.
With his seat in the meat
And his face in the fish
And his big hairy paws
In the buttery dish,
He's nibbling the noodles,
He's munching the rice,
He's slurping the soda,
He's licking the ice.
And he lets out a roar
If you open the door.
And it gives me a scare
To know he's in there—
That Polary Bear
In our Fridgitydaire.

47

## SUPERSTITIOUS

If you are superstitious you'll never step on cracks.
When you see a ladder you will never walk beneath it.
And if you ever spill some salt you'll throw some 'cross your back,
And carry 'round a rabbit's foot just in case you need it.
You'll pick up any pin that you find lying on the ground,
And never, never, ever throw your hat upon the bed,
Or open an umbrella when you are in the house.
You'll bite your tongue each time you say
A thing you shouldn't have said.
You'll hold your breath and cross your fingers
Walkin' by a graveyard,
And number thirteen's never gonna do you any good.
Black cats will all look vicious, if you're superstitious,
But I'm not superstitious (knock on wood).

## THE PIRATE

Oh, the blithery, blathery pirate
(His name, I believe, is Claude),
His manner is sullen and irate,
And his humor is vulgar and broad.

He has often been known to imprison
His friends in the hold dark and dank,
Or lash them up high on the mizzen,
Or force them to stroll down a plank.

He will selfishly ask you to dig up
Some barrels of ill-gotten gold,
And if you so much as just higgup,
He'll leave you to fill up the hole.

He may cast you adrift in a rowboat
(He has no reaction to tears)
Or put you ashore without NO boat
On an island and leave you for years.

He's a rotter, a wretch and a sinner,
He's foul as a fellow can be,
But if you invite him to dinner,
Oh, please sit him next to *me*!

## HURK

I'd rather play tennis than go to the dentist.
I'd rather play soccer than go to the doctor.
I'd rather play Hurk than go to work.
Hurk? Hurk? What's Hurk?
I don't know, but it *must* be better than work.

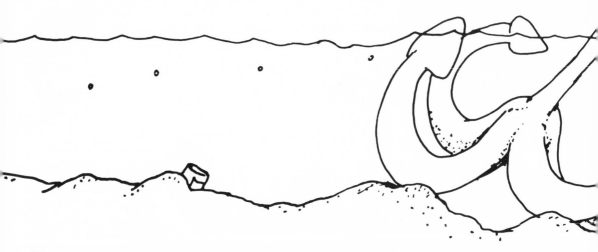

# ANCHORED

Our anchor's too big for our ship,
So we're sittin' here tryin' to think.
If we leave it behind we'll be lost.
If we haul it on board, we will sink.
If we sit and keep talkin' about it,
It will soon be too late for our trip.
It sure can be rough on a sailor
When the anchor's too big for the ship.

## UNSCRATCHABLE ITCH

There is a spot that you can't scratch
Right between your shoulder blades,
Like an egg that just won't hatch
Here you set and there it stays.
Turn and squirm and try to reach it,
Twist your neck and bend your back,
Hear your elbows creak and crack,
Stretch your fingers, now you bet it's
Going to reach—no that won't get it—
Hold your breath and stretch and pray,
Only just an inch away,
Worse than a sunbeam you can't catch
Is that one spot that
You can't scratch.

# SQUISHY TOUCH

Everything King Midas touched
Turned to gold, the lucky fellow.
Every single thing I touch
Turns to raspberry Jell-O.
Today I touched the kitchen wall (squish),
I went and punched my brother Paul (splish).
I tried to fix my bike last week (sploosh),
And kissed my mother on the cheek (gloosh).
I got into my overshoes (sklush),
I tried to read the Evening News (smush),
I sat down in the easy chair (splush),
I tried to comb my wavy hair (slush).
I took a dive into the sea (glush)—
Would you like to shake hands with me (sklush)?

# IMPORTNT?

Said little a to big G,
"Without me,
The sea would be
The se,
The flea would be
The fle.
And earth and heaven couldn't be
Without me."
Said big G to little a,
"Even the se
Could crsh nd spry,
Nd the fle would fly
In the sme old wy,
Nd erth nd heven still would be,
Without thee."

54

## THUMB FACE

There is a face upon my thumb—
I did not paint it there—
With pointy ears and winky eyes
And greenish bristly hair.
I keep it hidden from my friends
So that they will not stare.
It has a little twisty mouth,
And yellow teethies, too.
It snickers when I hold my fork,
It giggles when I'm blue,
And laughs and laughs and laughs
At everything I try to do.

# HOMEWORK MACHINE

The Homework Machine, oh the Homework Machine,
Most perfect contraption that's ever been seen.
Just put in your homework, then drop in a dime,
Snap on the switch, and in ten seconds' time,
Your homework comes out, quick and clean as can be.
Here it is—"nine plus four?" and the answer is "three."
Three?
Oh me . . .
I guess it's not as perfect
As I thought it would be.

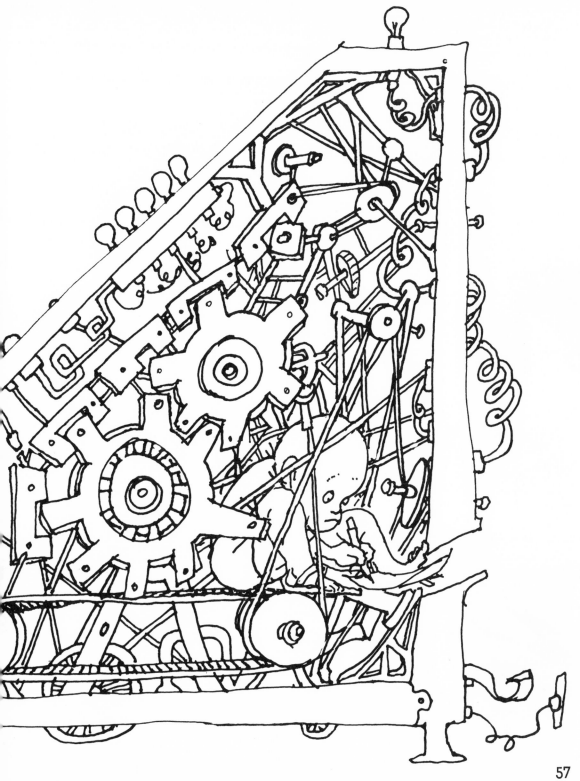

## EIGHT BALLOONS

Eight balloons no one was buyin'
All broke loose one afternoon.
Eight balloons with strings a-flyin',
Free to do what they wanted to.
One flew up to touch the sun—POP!
One thought highways might be fun—POP!
One took a nap in a cactus pile—POP!
One stayed to play with a careless child—POP!
One tried to taste some bacon fryin'—POP!
One fell in love with a porcupine—POP!
One looked close in a crocodile's mouth—POP!
One sat around 'til his air ran out—WHOOSH!
Eight balloons no one was buyin'—
They broke loose and away they flew,
Free to float and free to fly
And free to pop where they wanted to.

# ATIONS

If we meet and I say, "Hi,"
That's a salutation.
If you ask me how I feel,
That's consideration.
If we stop and talk awhile,
That's a conversation.
If we understand each other,
That's communication.
If we argue, scream and fight,
That's an altercation.
If later we apologize,
That's reconciliation.
If we help each other home,
That's cooperation.
And all these ations added up
Make civilization.

(And if I say this is a wonderful poem,
Is that exaggeration?)

# MUSICAL CAREER

She wanted to play the piano,
But her hands couldn't reach the keys.
When her hands could finally reach the keys,
Her feet couldn't reach the floor.
When her hands could finally reach the keys,
And her feet could reach the floor,
She didn't want to play that ol' piano anymore.

## ANTEATER

"A genuine anteater,"
The pet man told my dad.
Turned out, it was an *aunt* eater,
And now my uncle's mad!

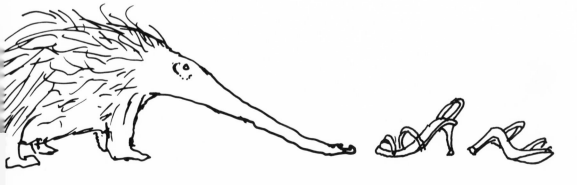

## BUCKIN' BRONCO

Can you ride the buckin' bronco?
Can you stay in that ol' saddle
Till your teeth begin to rattle?
Can you whoop and bounce
And stick upon his back?

Can you ride the buckin' bronco
While he's snortin' smoke and kickin'
And your stomach starts to sicken
And you feel as though
Your spine's about to crack?

I can ride the buckin' bronco,
I'll just sit up here and whistle
Till his strength begins to fizzle
And he knows that I'm
His master finally.

Yes I'll tame the buckin' bronco,
You can see me settin' easy.
Here's the buckin' bronco,

Here is me. →

RODEO

## SNAP!

She was opening up her umbrella,
She thought it was going to rain,
When we all heard a snap
Like the clap of a trap
And we never have seen her again.

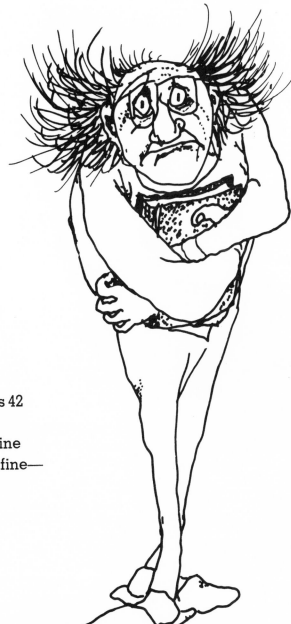

## OVERDUES

What do I do?
What do I do?
This library book is 42
Years overdue.
I admit that it's mine
But I can't pay the fine—
Should I turn it in
Or hide it again?
What do I do?
What do I do?

# WILD STRAWBERRIES

Are Wild Strawberries really wild?
Will they scratch an adult, will they snap at a child?
Should you pet them, or let them run free where they roam?
Could they ever relax in a steam-heated home?
Can they be trained to not growl at the guests?
Will a litterbox work or would they leave a mess?
Can we make them a Cowberry, herding the cows,
Or maybe a Muleberry pulling the plows,
Or maybe a Huntberry chasing the grouse,
Or maybe a Watchberry guarding the house,
And though they may curl up at your feet oh so sweetly,
Can you ever feel that you trust them completely?
Or should we make a pet out of something less scary,
Like the Domestic Prune or the Imported Cherry,
Anyhow, you've been warned and I will not be blamed
If your Wild Strawberry cannot be tamed.

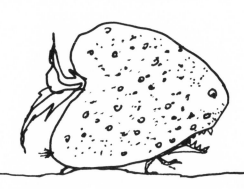

## HOW TO MAKE A SWING
## WITH NO ROPE
## OR BOARD OR NAILS

First grow a moustache
A hundred inches long,
Then loop it over a hick'ry limb
(Make sure the limb is strong).
Now pull yourself up off the ground
And wait until the spring—
Then swing!

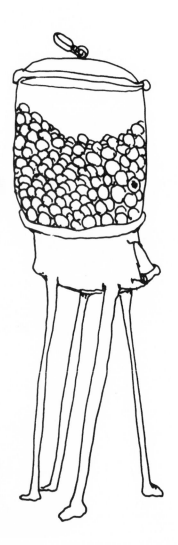

## GUMEYE BALL

There's an eyeball in the gumball machine,
Right there between the red and the green,
Lookin' at me as if to say,
"You don't need any more gum today."

# HOT DOG

I have a hot dog for a pet,
The only kind my folks would let
Me get.
He does smell sort of bad
And yet,
He absolutely never gets
The sofa wet.
We have a butcher for a vet,
The strangest vet you ever met.
Guess we're the weirdest family yet,
To have a hot dog for a pet.

## ADVENTURES OF A FRISBEE

The Frisbee, he got tired of sailing
To and fro and to;
And thought about the other things
That he might like to do.
So the next time that they threw him,
He turned there in the sky,
And sailed away to try and find
Some new things he could try.
He tried to be an eyeglass,
But no one could see through him.
He tried to be a UFO,
But everybody knew him.
He tried to be a dinner plate,
But he got cracked and quit.
He tried to be a pizza,
But got tossed and baked and bit.
He tried to be a hubcap,
But the cars all moved too quick.
He tried to be a record,
But the spinnin' made him sick.
He tried to be a quarter,
But he was too big to spend.
So he rolled home, quite glad to be
A Frisbee once again.

## COME SKATING

They said come skating;
They said it's so nice.
They said come skating;
I'd done it twice.
They said come skating;
It sounded nice. . . .
I wore roller—
They meant *ice*.

## THE MEEHOO WITH AN EXACTLYWATT

Knock knock!
    Who's there?
Me!
    Me who?
That's right!
    *What's* right?
Meehoo!
    *That's* what I want to know!
*What's* what you want to know?
    Me who?
Yes, exactly!
    Exactly *what*?
Yes, I have an Exactlywatt on a chain!
    Exactly *what* on a chain?
Yes!
    Yes *what*?
No, Exactlywatt!
    That's what I want to know!
I told you—Exactlywatt!
    Exactly *what*?
Yes!
    Yes what?
Yes, it's with me!
    *What's* with you?
Exactlywatt—that's what's with me.
    Me who?
Yes!
    Go away!

Knock knock . . .

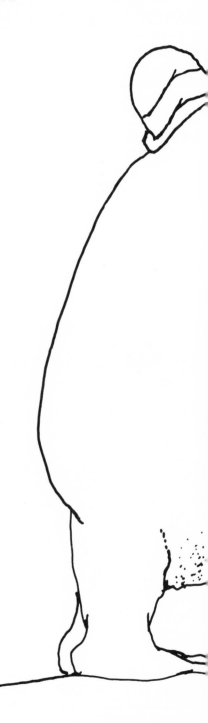

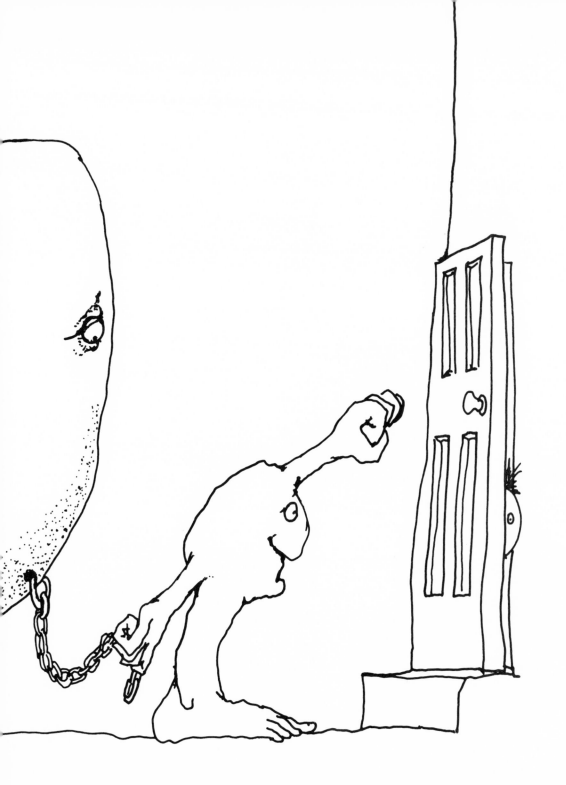

## CLOONY THE CLOWN

I'll tell you the story of Cloony the Clown
Who worked in a circus that came through town.
His shoes were too big and his hat was too small,
But he just wasn't, just wasn't funny at all.
He had a trombone to play loud silly tunes,
He had a green dog and a thousand balloons.
He was floppy and sloppy and skinny and tall,
But he just wasn't, just wasn't funny at all.
And every time he did a trick,
Everyone felt a little sick.
And every time he told a joke,
Folks sighed as if their hearts were broke.
And every time he lost a shoe,
Everyone looked awfully blue.
And every time he stood on his head,
Everyone screamed, "Go back to bed!"
And every time he made a leap,
Everybody fell asleep.
And every time he ate his tie,
Everyone began to cry.
And Cloony could not make any money
Simply because he *was not funny*.

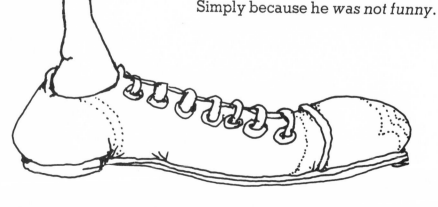

One day he said, "I'll tell this town
How it feels to be an unfunny clown."
And he told them all why he looked so sad,
And he told them all why he felt so bad.
He told of Pain and Rain and Cold,
He told of Darkness in his soul,
And after he finished his tale of woe,
Did everyone cry? Oh no, no, no,
They laughed until they shook the trees
With "Hah-Hah-Hahs" and "Hee-Hee-Hees."
They laughed with howls and yowls and shrieks,
They laughed all day, they laughed all week,
They laughed until they had a fit,
They laughed until their jackets split.
The laughter spread for miles around
To every city, every town,
Over mountains, 'cross the sea,
From Saint Tropez to Mun San Nee.
And soon the whole world rang with laughter,
Lasting till forever after,
While Cloony stood in the circus tent,
With his head drooped low and his shoulders bent.
And he said, "THAT IS NOT WHAT I MEANT—
I'M FUNNY JUST BY *ACCIDENT*."
And while the world laughed outside,
Cloony the Clown sat down and cried.

## TRYIN' ON CLOTHES

I tried on the farmer's hat,
Didn't fit.
A little too small—just a bit
Too floppy.
Couldn't get used to it,
Took it off.

I tried on the dancer's shoes,
A little too loose.
Not the kind you could use
For walkin'.
Didn't feel right in 'em,
Kicked 'em off.

I tried on the summer sun,
Felt good.
Nice and warm—knew it would.
Tried the grass beneath bare feet,
Felt neat.
Finally, finally felt well dressed,
Nature's clothes just fit me best.

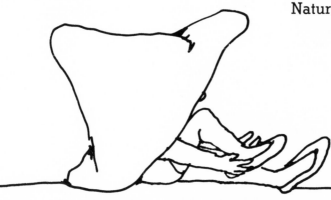

## SHAPES

A square was sitting quietly
Outside his rectangular shack
When a triangle came down—*kerplunk!*—
And struck him in the back.
"I must go to the hospital,"
Cried the wounded square,
So a passing rolling circle
Picked him up and took him there.

# TIRED

I've been working so hard you just wouldn't believe,
And I'm tired!
There's so little time and so much to achieve,
And I'm tired!
I've been lying here holding the grass in its place,
Pressing a leaf with the side of my face,
Tasting the apples to see if they're sweet,
Counting the toes on a centipede's feet.
I've been memorizing the shape of that cloud,
Warning the robins to not chirp so loud,
Shooing the butterflies off the tomatoes,
Keeping an eye out for floods and tornadoes.
I've been supervising the work of the ants
And thinking of pruning the cantaloupe plants,
Timing the sun to see what time it sets,
Calling the fish to swim into my nets,
And I've taken twelve thousand and forty-one breaths,
And  I'm  TIRED!

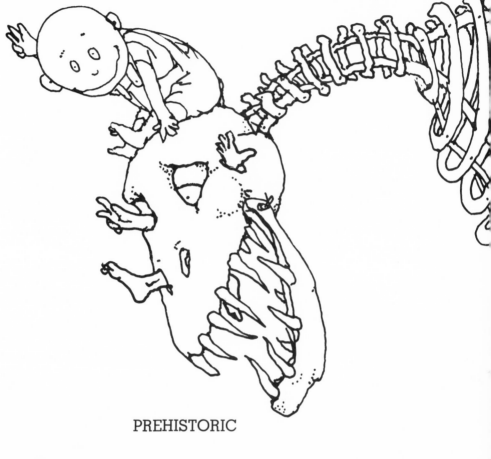

PREHISTORIC

These lizards, toads and turtles, dear, with which you love to play,
Were Dinosaurs and Plesiosaurs in prehistoric days.
They fought the armored Ankylosaurs and wild Brontosaurus,
Glyptodons and Varanids and hungry Plateosaurus.
Sharklike Ichthyosaurs and flying Pteranodon,
Tyrannosaurus, Kronosaurus and treacherous Trachodon.
Shrieking Archaeopteryx, Triceratops as well,
And those that I cannot pronounce, nor even try to spell.
But anyway, they slowly turned to lizards and turtles and snakes.
And all the brave and wild and woolly prehistoric *people*—
They turned into *us*, for goodness' sakes!

## MY GUITAR

Oh, wouldn't it be a most wondrous thing
To have a guitar that could play and could sing
By *itself*—what an absolute joy it would be
To have a guitar . . . that didn't need me.

## SPELLING BEE

I got stung by a bee
I won't tell you where.
I got stung by a bee
I was just lyin' there,
And it tattooed a message
I can't let you see
That spells out ·····

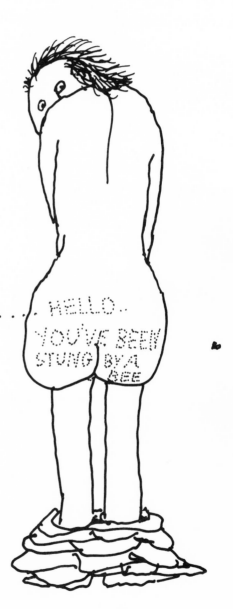

## ALWAYS SPRINKLE PEPPER

Always sprinkle pepper in your hair,
Always sprinkle pepper in your hair.
For then if you are kidnapped by a Wild Barbazzoop,
Who sells you to a Ragged Hag
Who wants you for her soup,
She'll pick you up and sniff you,
And then she'll sneeze "Achooo,"
And say, "My tot, you're much too hot,
I fear you'll never do."
And with a shout she'll throw you out,
And you'll run away from there,
And soon you will be safe at home a-sittin' in your chair,
If you always, always, always,
Always, always, always, always,
Always, always sprinkle pepper in your hair.

## PECKIN'

The saddest thing I ever did see
Was a woodpecker peckin' at a plastic tree.
He looks at me, and "Friend," says he,
"Things ain't as sweet as they used to be."

## IT'S HOT!

It's *hot!*
I can't get cool,
I've drunk a quart of lemonade.
I think I'll take my shoes off
And sit around in the shade.

It's *hot!*
My back is sticky,
The sweat rolls down my chin.
I think I'll take my clothes off
And sit around in my skin.

It's *hot!*
I've tried with 'lectric fans,
And pools and ice cream cones.
I think I'll take my skin off
And sit around in my bones.

It's *still* hot!

# TURTLE

Our turtle did not eat today,
Just lies on his back in the strangest way
And doesn't move.
I tickled him
And poked at him
And dangled string in front of him,
But he just lies there
Stiff and cold
And sort of staring straight ahead.
Jim says he's dead.
"Oh, no," say I,
"A wooden turtle cannot die!"

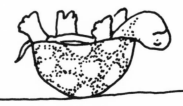

## CROWDED TUB

There's too many kids in this tub.
There's too many elbows to scrub.
I just washed a behind
That I'm sure wasn't mine,
There's too many kids in this tub.

## CHANNELS

Channel 1's no fun.
Channel 2's just news.
Channel 3's hard to see.
Channel 4 is just a bore.
Channel 5 is all jive.
Channel 6 needs to be fixed.
Channel 7 and Channel 8—
Just old movies, not so great.
Channel 9's a waste of time.
Channel 10 is off, my child.
Wouldn't you like to *talk* awhile?

## HIPPO'S HOPE

There once was a hippo who wanted to fly—
Fly-hi-dee, try-hi-dee, my-hi-dee-ho.
So he sewed him some wings that could flap through the sky—
Ski-hi-dee, fly-hi-dee, why-hi-dee-go.

He climbed to the top of a mountain of snow—
Snow-hi-dee, slow-hi-dee, oh-hi-dee-hoo.
With the clouds high above and the sea down below—
Where-hi-dee, there-hi-dee, scare-hi-dee-boo.

(Happy ending)
And he flipped and he flapped and he bellowed so loud—
Now-hi-dee, loud-hi-dee, proud-hi-dee-poop.
And he sailed like an eagle, off into the clouds—
High-hi-dee, fly-hi-dee, bye-hi-dee-boop.

(Unhappy ending)
And he leaped like a frog and he fell like a stone—
Stone-hi-dee, lone-hi-dee, own-hi-dee-flop.
And he crashed and he drowned and broke all his bones—
Bones-hi-dee, moans-hi-dee, groans-hi-dee-glop.

(Chicken ending)
He looked up at the sky and looked down at the sea—
Sea-hi-dee, free-hi-dee, whee-hi-dee-way.
And he turned and went home and had cookies and tea—
That's hi-dee, all hi-dee, I have to say.

# WHATIF

Last night, while I lay thinking here,
Some Whatifs crawled inside my ear
And pranced and partied all night long
And sang their same old Whatif song:
Whatif I'm dumb in school?
Whatif they've closed the swimming pool?
Whatif I get beat up?
Whatif there's poison in my cup?
Whatif I start to cry?
Whatif I get sick and die?
Whatif I flunk that test?
Whatif green hair grows on my chest?
Whatif nobody likes me?
Whatif a bolt of lightning strikes me?
Whatif I don't grow taller?
Whatif my head starts getting smaller?
Whatif the fish won't bite?
Whatif the wind tears up my kite?
Whatif they start a war?
Whatif my parents get divorced?
Whatif the bus is late?
Whatif my teeth don't grow in straight?
Whatif I tear my pants?
Whatif I never learn to dance?
Everything seems swell, and then
The nighttime Whatifs strike again!

## SOUR FACE ANN

Sour Face Ann,
With your chin in your hand,
Haven't you ever been pleased?
You used to complain
That you had no fur coat,
And now you complain of the fleas.

# THE CLIMBERS

A mountain climbing exploration
Took us to these distant peaks
Where no one's ever been before.
Was it my imagination?
Did I feel this mountain move?
Did I hear it snore?

## ROCKABYE

Rockabye baby, in the treetop.
Don't you know a treetop
Is no safe place to rock?
And who put you up there,
And your cradle too?
Baby, I think someone down here's
Got it in for you.

## THE LITTLE BOY AND THE OLD MAN

Said the little boy, "Sometimes I drop my spoon."
Said the little old man, "I do that too."
The little boy whispered, "I wet my pants."
"I do that too," laughed the little old man.
Said the little boy, "I often cry."
The old man nodded, "So do I."
"But worst of all," said the boy, "it seems
Grown-ups don't pay attention to me."
And he felt the warmth of a wrinkled old hand.
"I know what you mean," said the little old man.

## SURPRISE!

My Grandpa went to Myrtle Beach
And sent us back a turtle each.
And then he went to Katmandu
And mailed a real live Cockatoo.
From Rio an iguana came,
A smelly goat arrived from Spain.
Now he's in India, you see—
My Grandpa always thinks of me.

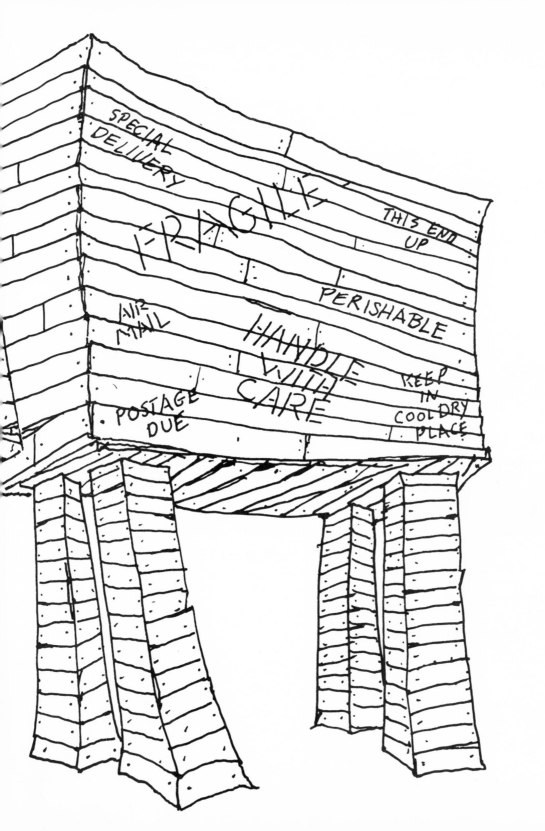

97

# TICKLISH TOM

Did you hear 'bout Ticklish Tom?
He got tickled by his mom.
Wiggled and giggled and fell on the floor,
Laughed and rolled right out the door.
All the way to school and then
He got tickled by his friends.
Laughed till he fell off his stool,
Laughed and rolled right out of school
Down the stairs and finally stopped
Till he got tickled by a cop.
And all the more that he kept gigglin',
All the more the folks kept ticklin'.
He shrieked and screamed and rolled around,
Laughed his way right out of town.
Through the country down the road,
He got tickled by a toad.
Past the mountains across the plain,
Tickled by the falling rain,
Tickled by the soft brown grass,
Tickled by the clouds that passed.
Giggling, rolling on his back
He rolled on the railroad track.
Rumble, rumble, whistle, roar—
Tom ain't ticklish anymore.

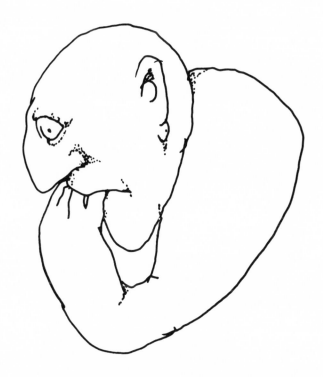

## THE NAILBITER

Some people manicure their nails,
Some people trim them neatly,
Some people keep them filed down,
I bite 'em off completely.
Yes, it's a nasty habit, but
Before you start to scold,
Remember, I have never ever
Scratched a single soul.

## THE FLY IS IN

The fly is in
The milk is in
The bottle is in
The fridge is in
The kitchen is in
The house is in
The town.

The flea is on
The dog is on
The quilt is on
The bed is on
The carpet is on
The floor is on
The ground.

The worm is under
The ground is under
The grass is under
The blanket is under
The diaper is under
The baby is under
The tree.

The bee is bothering
The puppy is bothering
The dog is bothering
The cat is bothering
The baby is bothering
Mama is bothering
Me.

## STRANGE WIND

What a strange wind it was today,
Whistlin' and whirlin' and scurlin' away
Like a worried old woman with so much to say.
What a strange wind it was today.

What a strange wind it was today,
Cool and clear from a sky so grey
And my hat stayed on but my head blew away—
What a strange wind it was today.

## ONE TWO

One two, buckle my shoe.

    "Buckle your *own* shoe!"

Who said that?

    "I did. What are you doing with those silly buckles on
    your shoes anyway?"

Three, four, shut the door.

    "You shut it—you *opened* it."

Er . . . five, six, pick up sticks.

    "Why should I pick them up—do you think I'm your
    slave? Buckle my shoe, shut the door, pick up sticks,
    next thing you'll be telling me to lay them straight."

But it's only a poem. . . . Nine, ten, a big fat . . . oh never mind.

## TUSK, TUSK

The Walrus got braces,
And that's why his face is
A tangle of wires and steel.
He'll sit and he'll wait
Till his tusks are both straight—
And then think how happy he'll feel!
(But meanwhile, they're ruining his meal.)

# CAPTAIN BLACKBEARD DID WHAT?

The sea is a-roarin', the sea gulls they screech,
The bosun he rants and he raves.
And the whole scurvy crew
Says, "It's true, yes it's true,
Ol' Captain Blackbeard's *shaved*."
We had buried some treasure (and bodies as well)
And was just sailin' back from the cave,
When he calls fer boiled water
And stomps down below
An' gor' but he comes up shaved.
There's a chickenish stubble, and fishbelly skin
On that face, once so blazin' and brave.
And his ol' faithful parrot
Can hardly bear it
Since ol' Captain Blackbeard shaved.
When he shouts, "Board and sink her!"
It sounds like a clinker
And gets lots of laughs from the slaves.
And his loud bawdy songs
Seem a little bit wrong
Since ol' Captain Blackbeard shaved.
Now no one is fearing his look or his lash
Or his threats of a watery grave.
And things ain't the same
In the piratin' game
Since ol' Captain Blackbeard shaved.

## MAGIC CARPET

You have a magic carpet
That will whiz you through the air,
To Spain or Maine or Africa
If you just tell it where.
So will you let it take you
Where you've never been before,
Or will you buy some drapes to match
And use it
On your
Floor?

## OUTSIDE OR UNDERNEATH?

Bob bought a hundred-dollar suit
But couldn't afford any underwear.
Says he, "If your outside looks real good
No one will know what's under there."

Jack bought some hundred-dollar shorts
But wore a suit with rips and tears.
Says he, "It won't matter what people see
As long as I know what's under there."

Tom bought a flute and a box of crayons,
Some bread and cheese and a golden pear.
And as for his suit or his underwear
He doesn't think about them much . . . or care.

# IT'S ALL THE SAME TO THE CLAM

You may leave the clam on the ocean's floor,
It's all the same to the clam.
For a hundred thousand years or more,
It's all the same to the clam.
You may bury him deep in mud and muck
Or carry him 'round to bring you luck,
Or use him for a hockey puck,
It's all the same to the clam.

You may call him Jim or Frank or Nell,
It's all the same to the clam.
Or make an ashtray from his shell,
It's all the same to the clam.
You may take him riding on the train
Or leave him sitting in the rain.
You'll never hear the clam complain,
It's all the same to the clam.

Yes, the world may stop or the world may spin,
It's all the same to the clam.
And the sky may come a-fallin' in,
It's all the same to the clam.
And man may sing his endless songs
Of wronging rights and righting wrongs.
The clam just sets—and gets along,
It's all the same to the clam.

## HULA EEL

Take an eel,
Make a loop,
Use him as a Hula Hoop.
Feel him twist and twirl and spin,
Down your ankles, round your chin,
Tighter, tighter, tighter yet,
Ain't an eel a lovely pet?
Hey—answer when I talk to you—
Don't just stand there turning blue.

## BORED

I can't afford
A skateboard.
I can't afford
An outboard.
I can't afford
A surfboard.
All I can afford
Is a board.

## STANDING IS STUPID

Standing is stupid,
Crawling's a curse,
Skipping is silly,
Walking is worse.
Hopping is hopeless,
Jumping's a chore,
Sitting is senseless,
Leaning's a bore.
Running's ridiculous,
Jogging's insane—
Guess I'll go upstairs and
Lie down again.

## WHO ORDERED THE BROILED FACE?

Well, here you are,
Just as you ordered,
Broiled face with butter sauce,
Mashed potatoes on the side.
What do you mean you wanted me *fried*?

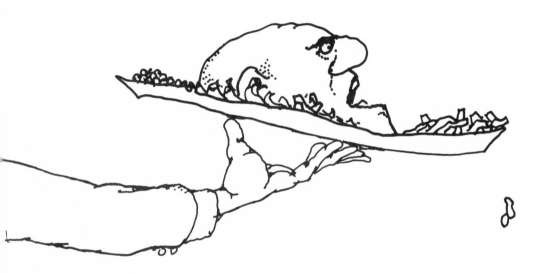

## THE MAN IN THE IRON PAIL MASK

He's the man in the iron pail mask,
He can do the most difficult task,
He can duel, he can joust,
He can charge, he can chase,
He can climb, he can rhyme,
He can wrestle and race.
He'll show you his courage
But never his face,
No matter how often you ask.
He's the Brave and the Fearless
The usually Tearless
Man in the iron pail mask.

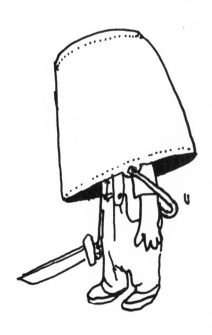

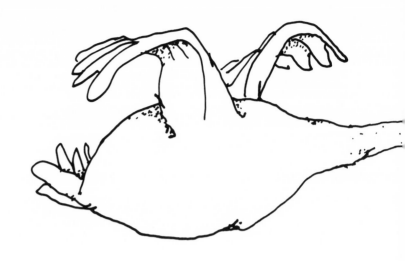

## GOOLOO

The Gooloo bird
She has no feet,
She cannot walk
Upon the street.
She cannot build
Herself a nest,
She cannot land
And take a rest.
Through rain and snow
And thunderous skies,
She weeps forever
As she flies,
And lays her eggs
High over town,
And prays that they
Fall safely down.

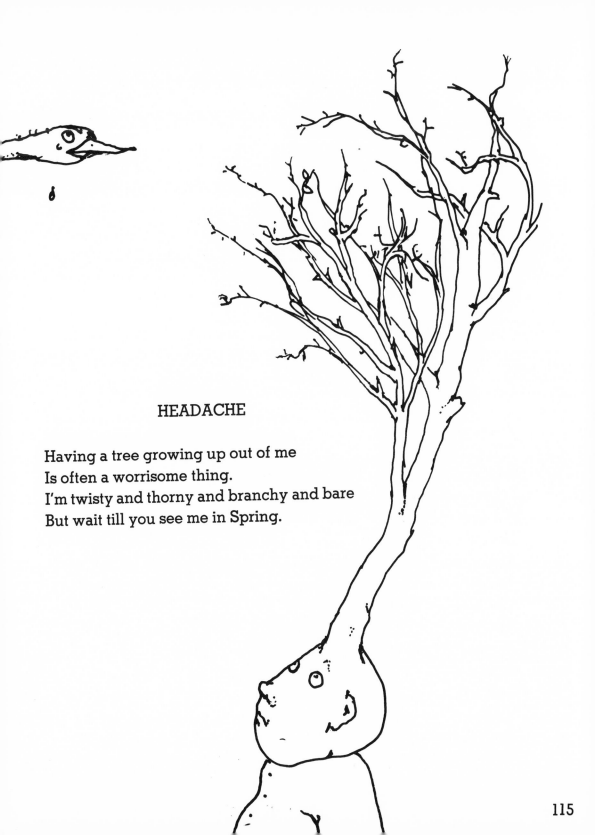

## HEADACHE

Having a tree growing up out of me
Is often a worrisome thing.
I'm twisty and thorny and branchy and bare
But wait till you see me in Spring.

# QUICK TRIP

We've been caught by the quick-digesting Gink,

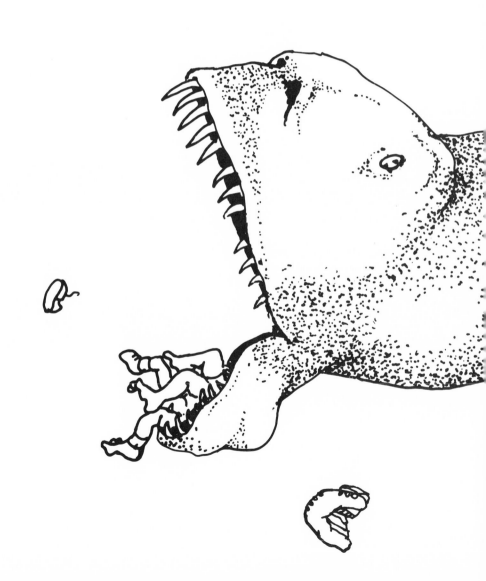

And now we are dodgin' his teeth . . .

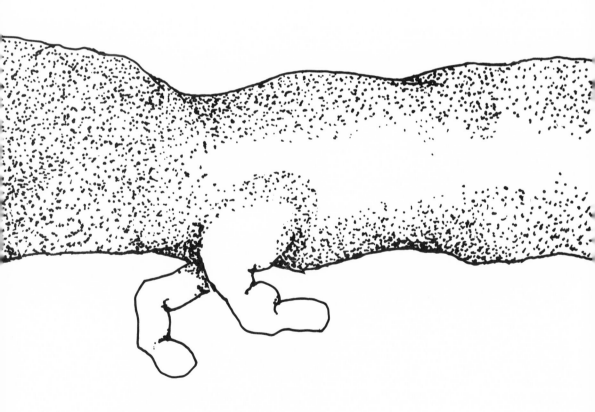

And now we are restin' in his intestine,

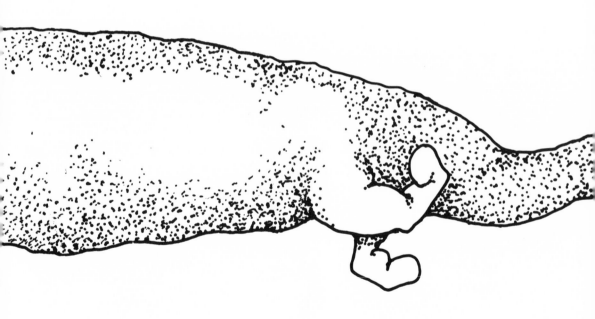

And now we're back out on the street.

# LITTLE ABIGAIL AND THE BEAUTIFUL PONY

THE PONY
THAT THEY
WOULDN'T
BUY ME.
. TOO LATE!

There was a girl named Abigail
Who was taking a drive
Through the country
With her parents
When she spied a beautiful sad-eyed
Grey and white pony.
And next to it was a sign
That said,
FOR SALE—CHEAP.
"Oh," said Abigail,
"May I have that pony?
May I please?"
And her parents said,
"No you may not."
And Abigail said,
"But I MUST have that pony."
And her parents said,
"Well, you can't have that pony,
But you can have a nice butter pecan
Ice cream cone when we get home."

And Abigail said,
"I don't want a butter pecan
Ice cream cone,
I WANT THAT PONY—
I MUST HAVE THAT PONY."
And her parents said,
"Be quiet and stop nagging—
You're *not* getting that pony."
And Abigail began to cry and said,
"If I don't get that pony I'll die."
And her parents said, "You won't die.
No child ever died yet from not getting a pony."
And Abigail felt so bad
That when they got home she went to bed,
And she couldn't eat,
And she couldn't sleep,
And her heart was broken,
And she DID die—
All because of a pony
That her parents wouldn't buy.

(This is a good story
To read to your folks
When they won't buy
You something you want.)

OH, IF SHE WERE ONLY ALIVE
I WOULD BUY HER A HUNDRED
A HUNDRED PONIES!

OH... WHAT FOOLS WE WERE.

121

## HICCUP CURE

Hic . . .
Hic . . .
Hic . . .
Hic . . .
Want to cure your hiccups quick?
Stick out your tongue and bite your lip.
Hold your breath and shake one hip,
Pull back your left foot and kick up.
Now, you see, we've cured your hiccup.
Nothing much to it—don't you feel swell?
Hic . . .
Oh well . . .

# THE PAINTER

I'm the man who paints the stripes upon the zebras,
And I also paint the warts upon the toad.
And with this brush and pot
I give leopards lovely spots
And add some color to the chipmunk's coat.

I paint the flamin' red on Robin Redbreast,
I pour the blue on bluegills by the shore.
And when the firefly's dim
I splash silver paint on him,
And he shines more brightly than he did before.

Jack Frost? He's just a part-time workin' fellah,
Touchin' up the leaves and trees and things.
He's famouser than me,
But I'm happier than he,
'Cause *I* paint the ones that runs—and flies—and sings!

# NOBODY

Nobody loves me,
Nobody cares,
Nobody picks me peaches and pears.
Nobody offers me candy and Cokes,
Nobody listens and laughs at my jokes.
Nobody helps when I get in a fight,
Nobody does all my homework at night.
Nobody misses me,
Nobody cries,
Nobody thinks I'm a wonderful guy.
So if you ask me who's my best friend, in a whiz,
I'll stand up and tell you that *Nobody* is.
But yesterday night I got quite a scare,
I woke up and Nobody just *wasn't there.*
I called out and reached out for Nobody's hand,
In the darkness where Nobody usually stands.
Then I poked through the house, in each cranny and nook,
But I found *somebody* each place that I looked.
I searched till I'm tired, and now with the dawn,
There's no doubt about it—
Nobody's *gone!*

## ZEBRA QUESTION

I asked the zebra,
Are you black with white stripes?
Or white with black stripes?
And the zebra asked me,
Are you good with bad habits?
Or are you bad with good habits?
Are you noisy with quiet times?
Or are you quiet with noisy times?
Are you happy with some sad days?
Or are you sad with some happy days?
Are you neat with some sloppy ways?
Or are you sloppy with some neat ways?
And on and on and on and on
And on and on he went.
I'll never ask a zebra
About stripes
Again.

## THE SWORD-SWALLOWER

The great sword-swallower Salomar,
He wears no ties or collars.
He leans back, opens up his mouth,
And "Gulp," his sword he swallers.

I guess he finds it fun to feel
That steel down in his belly.
It's fine for he, but as for me—
I'll take some bread and jelly.

## ARROWS

I shot an arrow toward the sky,
It hit a white cloud floating by.
The cloud fell dying to the shore,
I don't shoot arrows anymore.

# THE TOAD
## AND THE KANGAROO

Said the Toad to the Kangaroo,
"I can hop and so can you,
So if we marry we'll have a child
Who can jump a mountain or hop a mile
And we can call it a Toadaroo,"
Said the hopeful Toad to the Kangaroo.

Said the Kangaroo, "My dear,
What a perfectly lovely idea.
I would most gladly marry you,
But as for having a Toadaroo,
I'd rather we call it a Kangaroad,"
Said the Kangaroo to the frowning Toad.

So they argued but couldn't agree
On Rangatoo or Kangaree
And finally the Toad said, "I don't give a dang
If it's Rootakoad or Toadakang—
I really don't feel like marrying you!"
"Fine with me," said the Kangaroo.

And the Toad had no more to say,
And the Kangaroo just hopped away.
And they never married or had a child
That could jump a mountain or hop a mile.
What a loss—what a shame—
Just 'cause they couldn't agree on a name.

PLAY BALL

Okay, let's play, I think that we
Have everyone we need.
I'll be the strong-armed pitcher
Who can throw with blinding speed.
And Pete will be the catcher
Who squats low and pounds his mitt,
And Mike will be the home-run king
Who snarls and waits to hit
One, loud and long and hard and high,
Way out beyond the wall.
So let's get start— What? *You?* Oh, yes,
You can be the ball!

## FRIENDSHIP

I've discovered a way to stay friends forever—
There's really nothing to it.
I simply tell you what to do
And you do it!

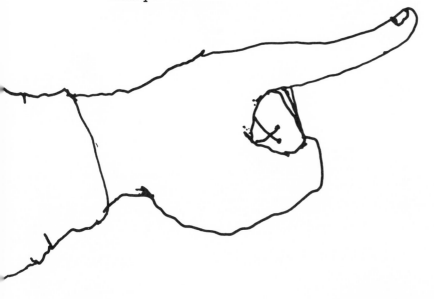

## EXAMINATION

I went to the doctor—
He reached down my throat,
He pulled out a shoe
And a little toy boat,
He pulled out a skate
And a bicycle seat,
And said, "Be more careful
About what you eat."

## POEMSICLE

If you add sicle to your pop,
Would he become a Popsicle?
Would a mop become a mopsicle?
Would a cop become a copsicle?
Would a chop become a chopsicle?
Would a drop become a dropsicle?
Would a hop become a hopsicle?
I guess it is time to stopsicle,
Or is it timesicle to stopsicle?
Heysicle, I can't stopsicle.
Ohsicle mysicle willsicle Isicle
Havesicle tosicle talksicle
Likesicle thissicle foreversicle—
Huhsicle?

## SENSES

A Mouth was talking to a Nose and an Eye.
A passing listening Ear
Said, "Pardon me, but you spoke so loud,
I couldn't help but overhear."
But the Mouth just closed and the Nose turned up
And the Eye just looked away,
And the Ear with nothing more to hear
Went sadly on its way.

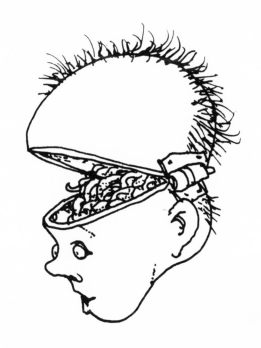

## HINGES

If we had hinges on our heads
There wouldn't be no sin,
'Cause we could take the bad stuff out
And leave the good stuff in.

## FEAR

Barnabus Browning
Was scared of drowning,
So he never would swim
Or get into a boat
Or take a bath
Or cross a moat.
He just sat day and night
With his door locked tight
And the windows nailed down,
Shaking with fear
That a wave might appear,
And cried so many tears
That they filled up the room
And he drowned.

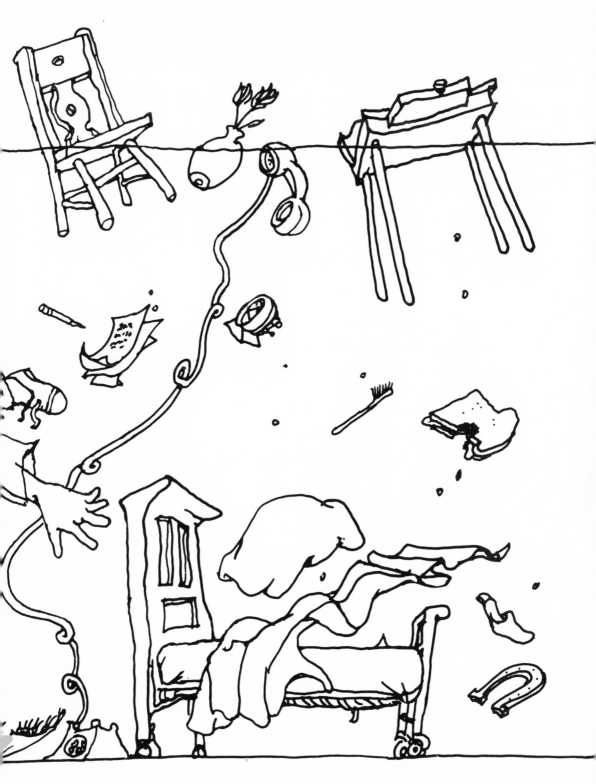

137

## TWISTABLE, TURNABLE MAN

He's the Twistable Turnable Squeezable Pullable
Stretchable Foldable Man.
He can crawl in your pocket or fit in your locket
Or screw himself into a twenty-volt socket,
Or stretch himself up to the steeple or taller,
Or squeeze himself into a thimble or smaller,
Yes he can, course he can,
He's the Twistable Turnable Squeezable Pullable
Stretchable Shrinkable Man.
And he lives a passable life
With his Squeezable Lovable Kissable Hugable
Pullable Tugable Wife.
And they have two twistable kids
Who bend up the way that they did.
And they turn and they stretch
Just as much as they can
For this Bendable Foldable
Do-what-you're-toldable
Easily moldable
Buy-what you're-soldable
Washable Mendable
Highly dependable
Buyable Saleable
Always available
Bounceable Shakable
Almost unbreakable
Twistable Turnable Man.

## BATTY

The baby bat
Screamed out in fright,
"Turn on the dark,
I'm afraid of the light."

## HITTING

Use a log to hit a hog.
Use a twig to hit a pig.
Use a rake to hit a snake.
Use a swatter to hit an otter.
Use a ski to hit a bee.
And use a feather when you hit me.

## CATCHING

I tried to catch a cold
As he went running past
On a damp and chilly
Afternoon in autumn.
I tried to catch a cold,
But he skittered by so fast
That I missed him—
But I'm glad to hear *you* caught him.

# DEAF DONALD

Deaf Donald met Talkie Sue

But  was all he could do.

And Sue said, "Donald, I sure do like you."

But  was all he could do.

And Sue asked Donald, "Do you like me too?"

But  was all he could do.

"Good-bye then, Donald, I'm leaving you."

But  was all he did do.

And she left forever so she never knew

That  means I love you.

## HAVE FUN

It's safe to swim
In Pemrose Park.
I guarantee
There are no sharks.

## DOG'S DAY

They could have sung me just one song
To kind of sort of celebrate.
Or left a present on the lawn—
A juicy bone, a piece of steak—
Instead of just a candle on
This lump of dog food on my plate.
But no one cares when a dog was born,
And this ain't much of a birthday cake.

## SKIN STEALER

This evening I unzipped my skin
And carefully unscrewed my head,
Exactly as I always do
When I prepare myself for bed.
And while I slept a coo-coo came
As naked as could be
And put on the skin
And screwed on the head
That once belonged to me.
Now wearing my feet
He runs through the street
In a most disgraceful way,
Doin' things and sayin' things
I'd never do or say,
Ticklin' the children
And kickin' the men
And dancin' the ladies away.
So if he makes your bright eyes cry
Or makes your poor head spin,
That scoundrel you see
Is not really me—
He's the coo-coo
Who's wearing my skin.

# LADIES FIRST

Pamela Purse yelled, *"Ladies first,"*
Pushing in front of the ice cream line.
Pamela Purse yelled, *"Ladies first,"*
Grabbing the ketchup at dinnertime.
Climbing on the morning bus
She'd shove right by all of us
And there'd be a tiff or a fight or a fuss
When Pamela Purse yelled, *"Ladies first."*

Pamela Purse screamed, *"Ladies first,"*
When we went off on our jungle trip.
Pamela Purse said her thirst was worse
And guzzled our water, every sip.
And when we got grabbed by that wild savage band,
Who tied us together and made us all stand
In a long line in front of the King of the land—
A cannibal known as Fry-'Em-Up Dan,
Who sat on his throne in a bib so grand
With a lick on his lips and a fork in his hand,
As he tried to decide who'd be first in the pan—
From back of the line, in that shrill voice of hers,
Pamela Purse yelled, *"Ladies first."*

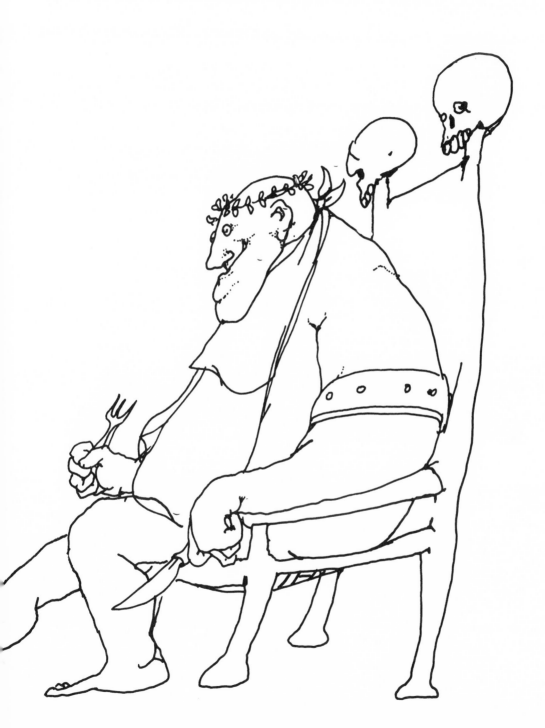

## FROZEN DREAM

I'll take the dream I had last night
And put it in my freezer,
So someday long and far away
When I'm an old grey geezer,
I'll take it out and thaw it out,
This lovely dream I've frozen,
And boil it up and sit me down
And dip my old cold toes in.

## THE LOST CAT

We can't find the cat,
We don't know where she's at,
Oh, where did she go?
Does anyone know?
Let's ask this walking hat.

## GOD'S WHEEL

God says to me with kind of a smile,
"Hey how would you like to be God awhile
And steer the world?"
"Okay," says I, "I'll give it a try.
Where do I set?
How much do I get?
What time is lunch?
When can I quit?"
"Gimme back that wheel," says God,
"I don't think you're quite ready yet."

## SHADOW RACE

Every time I've raced my shadow
When the sun was at my back,
It always ran ahead of me,
Always got the best of me.
But every time I've raced my shadow
When my face was toward the sun,
I won.

# CLARENCE

Clarence Lee from Tennessee
Loved the commercials he saw on TV.
He watched with wide believing eyes
And bought everything they advertised—
Cream to make his skin feel better,
Spray to make his hair look wetter,
Bleach to make his white things whiter,
Stylish jeans that fit much tighter.
Toothpaste for his cavities,
Powder for his doggie's fleas,
Purple mouthwash for his breath,
Deodorant to stop his sweat.
He bought each cereal they presented,
Bought each game that they invented.
Then one day he looked and saw
"A brand-new Maw, a better Paw!
New, improved in every way—
Hurry, order yours today!"
So, of course, our little Clarence
Sent off for two brand-new parents.
The new ones came in the morning mail,
The old ones he sold at a garage sale.
And now they all are doing fine:
His new folks treat him sweet and kind,
His old ones work in an old coal mine.
So if your Maw and Paw are mean
And make you eat your lima beans
And make you wash and make you wait
And never let you stay up late
And scream and scold and preach and pout,
That simply means they're wearing out.
So send off for two brand-new parents
And you'll be as happy as little Clarence.

155

## RHINO PEN

Tell me then,
Of all you've seen,
What could be more preposterous
Than forgetting your pen
And writing a theme
With
The
Horn
Of
A
Patient
Rhinoceros?

# IF

If I had wheels instead of feet
And roses 'stead of eyes
Then I could drive to the flower show
And maybe win a prize.

# PUSH BUTTON

I push the light switch button and—*click*—the light goes on.
I push the lawn mower button and—*voom*—it mows the lawn.
I push the root beer button and—*whoosh*—it fills my cup.
I push the glove compartment button—*clack*—it opens up.
I push the TV button and—*zap*—there's Wyatt Earp.
I push my belly button . . .
*BURP!*

# KIDNAPPED!

This morning I got kidnapped
By three masked men.
They stopped me on the sidewalk,
And offered me some candy,
And when I wouldn't take it
They grabbed me by the collar,
And pinned my arms behind me,
And shoved me in the backseat
Of this big black limousine and
Tied my hands behind my back
With sharp and rusty wire.
Then they put a blindfold on me
So I couldn't see where they took me,
And plugged up my ears with cotton
So I couldn't hear their voices.
And drove for 20 miles or
At least for 20 minutes, and then
Dragged me from the car down to
Some cold and moldy basement,
Where they stuck me in a corner
And went off to get the ransom
Leaving one of them to guard me
With a shotgun pointed at me,
Tied up sitting on a stool . . .
That's why I'm late for school!

## SUSPENSE

Oh Murdering Jack
Tied Louise to the track
In a plan that was grisly and gory,
While back in the shack
Was her Marvelous Mack,
Held prisoner there by the Outlaw Suntory.
Then the wolf pack attacked
And then down from the stack
With six-guns ablaze jumped young Billy McClory.
A CRASH! And a CRY! And I'm sorry but I
Have forgotten the rest of the story. .

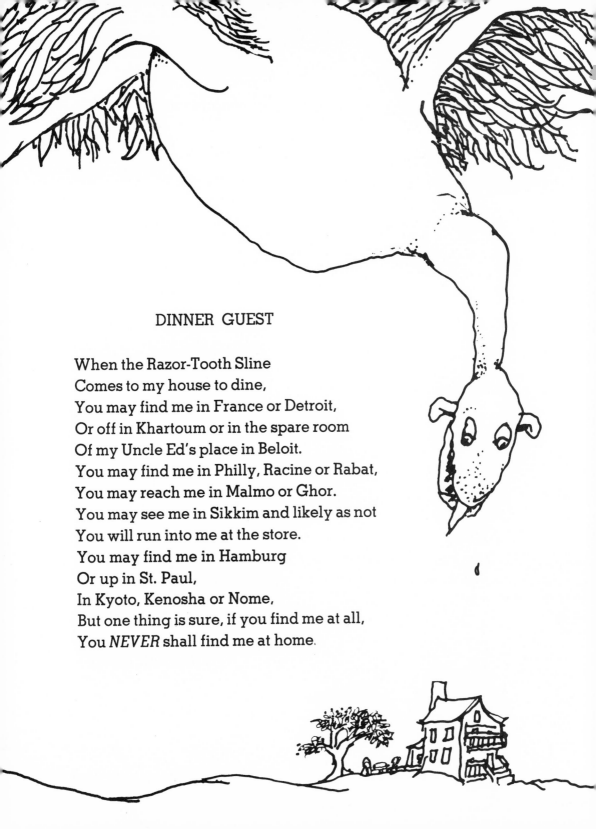

## DINNER GUEST

When the Razor-Tooth Sline
Comes to my house to dine,
You may find me in France or Detroit,
Or off in Khartoum or in the spare room
Of my Uncle Ed's place in Beloit.
You may find me in Philly, Racine or Rabat,
You may reach me in Malmo or Ghor.
You may see me in Sikkim and likely as not
You will run into me at the store.
You may find me in Hamburg
Or up in St. Paul,
In Kyoto, Kenosha or Nome,
But one thing is sure, if you find me at all,
You *NEVER* shall find me at home.

## IN SEARCH OF CINDERELLA

From dusk to dawn,
From town to town,
Without a single clue,
I seek the tender, slender foot
To fit this crystal shoe.
From dusk to dawn,
I try it on
Each damsel that I meet.
And I still love her so, but oh,
I've started hating feet.

# ALMOST PERFECT

"Almost perfect . . . but not quite."
Those were the words of Mary Hume
At her seventh birthday party,
Looking 'round the ribboned room.
"This tablecloth is *pink* not *white*—
Almost perfect . . . but not quite."

"Almost perfect . . . but not quite."
Those were the words of grown-up Mary
Talking about her handsome beau,
The one she wasn't gonna marry.
"Squeezes me a bit too tight—
Almost perfect . . . but not quite."

"Almost perfect . . . but not quite."
Those were the words of ol' Miss Hume
Teaching in the seventh grade,
Grading papers in the gloom
Late at night up in her room.
"They never cross their t's just right—
Almost perfect . . . but not quite."

Ninety-eight the day she died
Complainin' 'bout the spotless floor.
People shook their heads and sighed,
"Guess that she'll like heaven more."
Up went her soul on feathered wings,
Out the door, up out of sight.
Another voice from heaven came—
"Almost perfect . . . but not quite."

## PIE PROBLEM

If I eat one more piece of pie, I'll die!
If I can't have one more piece of pie, I'll die!
So since it's all decided I must die,
I might as well have one more piece of pie.
MMMM—OOOH—MY!
Chomp—Gulp—'Bye.

## THE OAK AND THE ROSE

An oak tree and a rosebush grew,
Young and green together,
Talking the talk of growing things—
Wind and water and weather.
And while the rosebush sweetly bloomed
The oak tree grew so high
That now it spoke of newer things—
Eagles, mountain peaks and sky.
"I guess you think you're pretty great,"
The rose was heard to cry,
Screaming as loud as it possibly could
To the treetop in the sky.
"And you have no time for flower talk,
Now that you've grown so tall."
"It's not so much that I've grown," said the tree,
"It's just that you've stayed so small."

# THEY'VE PUT A BRASSIERE ON THE CAMEL

They've put a brassiere on the camel,
She wasn't dressed proper, you know.
They've put a brassiere on the camel
So that her humps wouldn't show.
And they're making other respectable plans,
They're even insisting the pigs should wear pants,
They'll dress up the ducks if we give them the chance
Since they've put a brassiere on the camel.

They've put a brassiere on the camel,
They claim she's more decent this way.
They've put a brassiere on the camel,
The camel had nothing to say.
They squeezed her into it, I'll never know how,
They say that she looks more respectable now,
Lord knows what they've got in mind for the cow,
Since they've put a brassiere on the camel.

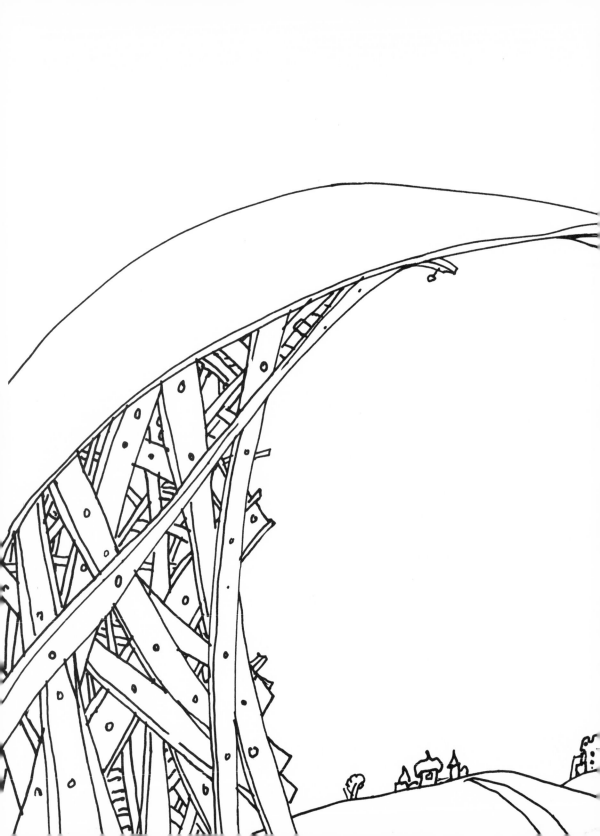

## THIS BRIDGE

This bridge will only take you halfway there
To those mysterious lands you long to see:
Through gypsy camps and swirling Arab fairs
And moonlit woods where unicorns run free.
So come and walk awhile with me and share
The twisting trails and wondrous worlds I've known.
But this bridge will only take you halfway there—
The last few steps you'll have to take alone.

# INDEX

For their help in the preparation of this book,
my deepest thanks to Charlotte Zolotow,
Joan Robins, Robert Warren, Jim Skofield,
Glenise Butcher and John Vitale.
And forever to Ursula Nordstrom. . . .

*Shel Silverstein*

Book and jacket design by Kim Llewellyn.